THE ASSURED EXPECTATION OF THINGS HOPED FOR

a novella

SHAWN MIHALIK

Asymmetrical Press
Missoula, Montana

Published by Asymmetrical Press, Missoula, Montana.

This book is a work of fiction. All characters in this book are completely imagined (although if you really tried, you could probably find parallels to people the author knows or knew at some point in his life—that's often how fiction works).

Library of Congress Cataloging-In-Publication Data
The assured expectation of things hoped for / Shawn Mihalik — 1st ed.
ISBN: 978-1-68287-000-6
eISBN: 978-1-68287-001-3
1. Jehovah's Witnesses. 2. Religion. 3. Shunning. 4. Excommunication. 5. Coming of age.

Cover design by Colin Wright
Formatted in beautiful Montana
Printed in the U.S.A.

Publisher info:
Website: www.asymmetrical.co
Email: howdy@asymmetrical.co
Twitter: @asympress

ASYM
METR
ICAL

For Stefan and Lauren and all the rest.
I love you.

Faith is the assured expectation of things hoped for,
the evident demonstration of realities though not beheld.

—Hebrews 11:1

The Assured Expectation of Things Hoped For

I REMEMBER KRISTY KELLY.

I think everyone else remembers her too, even if they pretend they don't. Even if they pretend, like we're supposed to, that she never existed, that she wasn't one of us and that she didn't talk to us and try to smile at us even though she was never really feeling it.

I always had a sort of crush on her, from the time we were very small—I was six and she eight, and I wonder sometimes if my fondness for her at that age was stoked by the years she had on me, by the experience that came from having braces (when I saw her braces I wanted braces so she could see that I was mature like she was, mature enough for braces), by the experience that came from having an Elder as a father, the experience that came from having a father, from having a mother and from having, at one point, a whole family.

The last time I saw Kristy Kelly was a few years ago, at the wedding. Most people who attended that wedding pretended she wasn't there. They pretended they didn't see her in the back corner of the hotel ballroom, looking cold and uncomfortable, knowing she didn't belong there. They pretended she didn't come for the ceremony and then leave after not even a hug from the bride or groom.

I pretend, too, because I'm supposed to. We all pretend so that we might bring them back. It's a kindness. An act of love. We do not speak of those who are like the dead. And we do not act as if we remember.

But I remember Kristy Kelly. I remember her.

THE LAST TIME I SPOKE to Kristy Kelly (which was not at the wedding; nobody spoke to Kristy Kelly at the wedding) she told me about the first time she experienced doubt about the religion into which she'd been born.

She was seven years old and it was the day of her brother's baptism.

Jehovah's Witnesses aren't baptized in infancy. We wait until we're older, until we can decide for ourselves whether we're ready to dedicate our lives to God, because that sort of dedication is a commitment that should not be taken lightly. There are consequences to dedication. And there are consequences to breaking dedication. There are, if you break your dedication by doing something that displeases God, repercussions.

Excommunication, shunning, the cutting of all ties with friends and family still in the organization, the crushing weight of the outside world, eternal death and damnation with the rest of wicked man come Armageddon: these are the things that happen if you break your vow.

Kristy's brother was twelve.

Kristy sat next to her mother in the bleachers of the Wolstein Center, which, instead of hosting hockey matches or rock concerts that weekend, had been appropriated for this massive three-day gathering. With her mother and her father and 6,000 other Jehovah's Witnesses Kristy listened as her brother and the others waiting with him to be baptized in water on that day were by that gray-haired Brother on the platform asked two questions:

"One," the Brother, an Elder, said in a sonorous voice amplified by stadium speakers, "on the basis of the sacrifice of Jesus Christ, have you repented of your sins and dedicated yourself to Jehovah to do his will?"

Kristy watched and heard her twelve-year-old brother and the fifty or so others with him answer, firmly and soundly: "Yes!"

"Two," the Brother said, "do you understand that your dedication and baptism identify you as one of Jehovah's Witnesses in association with God's spirit-direct organization?"

Her brother, with the others, again said: "Yes!"

And the Elder on the platform said: "Your clear, affirmative answers to those questions give evidence that you are qualified for baptism as ordained ministers of Jehovah God." And then he said a prayer.

Okay, so Kristy didn't actually experience doubt when she heard her brother asked these questions, but later she did, and she told me she should have on that day. She wished she had.

"Twelve years old," she said to me. "Twelve years old and in an almost legal way binding himself to the whim of an organization. And I did it too, a few years later. And so did you, a few years after me. It's just fucked up, when I finally stopped to think about it."

Is it?
I don't know.
Maybe.
I don't know.

KRISTY KELLY WAS WHAT WE call a born-in. Her family on her mother's side had been one of Jehovah's people since back in the early 1900s, and her father's father was baptized in 1969.

When Kristy was seven, not long before her brother's baptism, her dad was appointed an Elder, one of the heads of the congregation. Elder is not a title. Kristy's father was not "Elder Kelly," still Brother Kelly as he'd always been, as the other males (adult men, teenage boys, even children and toddlers) in the congregation are. But now he was one of the heads of the congregation.

It's stressful having an Elder for a father, Kristy told me. Suddenly everything his children did reflected on him. He could not shepherd God's flock if he couldn't shepherd first his family.

"I think that's why my brother got baptized when he did."

"KRISTY KELLY," THE PRINCIPAL SAID as he pulled the paper from the envelope. He didn't even read it. He knew who they had chosen. They all knew. She was the obvious choice. They probably needn't even have voted.

There was applause and celebratory feet-stomping and whoops and hollers as Kristy stood, walked to the school auditorium's wood-paneled stage.

"Students," the principal said. He took Kristy's hand, held it high. "Your new class president."

Whoops and hollers and celebratory foot-stomping.

WHEN KRISTY KELLY, THIRTEEN YEARS old and in seventh grade and ecstatic at having been chosen to lead her class, went home that day and told her parents and her brother the news, they were all very sad.

Well, her brother wasn't so much sad as he was inexpressive, glazed.

But her parents were sad.

How had this happened?

How did you let this happen? her mother asked her father.

How did I—? How did—?

And then her mother said she shouldn't have said that. She was sorry. They needed to deal with this together.

And Kristy sat on the living room sofa where they'd told her to sit, books open, notebooks open, doing homework: sums and equations.

Sums and equations.

Kristy wondered what was going on, although really she knew.

She'd been excited when the principal announced the holding of class elections. People at school liked Kristy, but they didn't really *like* her. She didn't stand during home room for the Pledge of Allegiance. She always declined the cupcakes and candies other students brought to share on their birthdays. She ate lunch with a couple other girls (but no boys, because her middle school had an official policy of gender segregation during lunch), but she didn't do anything with them outside of school, didn't go to their birthday parties or the PTA-sponsored all-night cosmic skate events at the local roller rink. When one of her classes watched a movie and that class was History and the movie was something like *Schindler's List* or the class was Music and the movie was the R-rated director's cut of *Amadeus*, Kristy was excused with a note from her parents and spent the class period in the library. She spent School Spirit Rallies in the library, too.

So what Kristy thought when the principal announced the class elections was that, if she were class president, it would be a thing for her to do: a normal thing.

And of course she knew, even when her name was called, it wouldn't fly.

Kristy's parents walked into the living room. Her father sat in front of her on the coffee table, facing her, crushing her math book, her sums and equations. Her mother remained standing with folded arms and drawn shoulders and angry hips.

"Kristy," her father said.

Sums and equations. He was crushing them.

"Kristy," her father said, "can you go get your Bible for me?"

"I don't want to," Kristy said.

From her mother came a gasp. Hand over mouth. Tear?

"Okay. Well I have mine right here. And so let's look at something Jesus said, honey."

Kristy's father's Bible was a mythical thing to her: Like all Jehovah's Witnesses' Bibles it was a *New World Translation* (Revised Standard Edition (c) 1986—although a new version has been published since this story's end, because the light gets ever brighter, the message always clearer), but unlike most Jehovah's Witnesses' it was dark blue leather with a gilded edge and gilded lettering on front of the blue leather. Its cover was cracked and worn but sturdy (not unlike Kristy's father himself), its built-in bookmark ribbon frayed but strong. "Your grandfather gave this to me when I got baptized, when I was sixteen, and I'll get one like it for you when you dedicate yourself, too, whatever color you like." Kristy's brother had one like it now, but Kristy's brother's didn't have the decades of hand-written notes and marginalia her father's did.

"Do you see this scripture there?" her father said, holding the Bible out to her, crushing her sums and equations and dreams of being like everybody else. "Read that for me. There. Verse 14."

Kristy read: "'I have given your word to them, but the world has hated them, because they are no part of the world, just as I am no part of the world.'"

"Thank you, Kristy. And do you know who said that?"

Oh, she knew, but she wasn't talking.

But apparently they weren't talking either, not until she did, so she said: "Jesus."

"Jesus."

Kristy's mother's arms had returned to the closed position. Closed to all.

"Do we vote?" her father asked.

Kristy shook her head.

"Do we take any part in elections?"

"No."

"Because…?"

"Because God's Kingdom."

"What about God's Kingdom?"

"We support God's Kingdom, not man's rulership."

"Exactly."

"But this is *school*. It's not real."

Kristy's mother made a sound. The sound was like a *harumph*.

And in that moment Kristy's brother came from his room upstairs in a leather jacket and with a baseball cap askew on his head and passed necessarily through the living room.

"Where are you going?" Kristy's mother said.

"Out," her brother said.

"It's family worship night," her father said.

"Well, and I have plans, so I'm going out."

And he went out and shut the door behind himself and in the evening stillness they could hear him start his car and then drive away.

Kristy's mother's arms went from closed to akimbo and she glared at Kristy's father. "Well what are you going to do about that?"

"I—"

"It's shit," Kristy's mother said. "Shit. Shit."

"You should go finish you homework in your room, Kristy," her father said.

Jehovah's Witnesses aren't supposed to swear. Jesus didn't swear and the Apostle Paul spoke specifically against it. But God knows nobody's perfect, and he forgives things like that, sometimes.

LATER THAT NIGHT, AFTER A lot of yelling, Kristy's father came into her room and read her that scripture again. He asked her if she understood and she said she did and he told her she had to tell the principal the next day that she couldn't be the class president. She said she would.

Her father told her he was proud of her.

God was proud of her.

Her brother came home that night smelling of cigarettes.

Kristy didn't make any friends at school for years after that.

BUT THAT WAS OKAY: NOT having any friends at school. They wouldn't have been valuable anyway—they wouldn't have been *real* friends.

There's a video that came out when I was young (and thus also when Kristy Kelly was young, although not as young as I was), called *Young People Ask: How Can I Make Real Friends?*

Young People Ask, before it was a video, was a book, and before it was a book it was a series of articles in the *Awake!* magazine, all (the book, the video, the articles and the magazine) published by Jehovah's Witnesses. Valuable publications, these were. Sage advice from the Bible on things like school and recreation and dating and masturbation and obeying your parents and why you shouldn't engage in premarital sex and what exactly constitutes sex (pretty much everything constitutes sex). I actually started reading the book way before I knew what masturbation was. I masturbated just once, after I read about it in the book, before I got to the part about it being unclean and probably, when you really think about it, selfish.

The video, *How Can I Make Real Friends?*, was about this teenage girl who moves from her old congregation with her family to a new one in New York City where she knows nobody and where nobody knows her and where there's nobody her own age. But some kids at her new school take an interest in her. They're a nice group, these kids. Kind. Generous. Fun. The teenage girl likes them. They show her the city, and in Times Square or somewhere they all watch this mime put on a show, and they all laugh and have a good time and the teenage girl likes them. But then they offer her drugs. And then one of the boys tries to have sex with her.

When I was ten my mom and Kristy's parents and some of the other parents in the area congregations got their kids all together with cookies and soda to watch the video and discuss it afterwards.

Kristy was kind of like the girl in the video. She wasn't new to our city or anything, but in our congregation there were no girls her age, no girls even close to her age, only boys, like me and Dan Herschel and Charlie Wallace.

"You should make arrangements to preach with Sister Davies," Kristy's mother said to her one day.

"But Sister Davies is old," Kristy said.

Sister Davies wasn't that old, maybe forty-five, maybe fifty, but she was unmarried, never married, and her devotion was to God.

What Kristy didn't know was that her mother had already spoken with Sister Davies on her behalf. Had made the arrangements. Had said Kristy wanted to preach with Sister Davies.

So the next rainy Saturday Kristy walked from door to door with Sister Davies, a flower-patterned canvas bag full of *Watchtowers* slung over her shoulder.

First Sister Davies told Kristy she was glad for the opportunity to get to know Kristy better. "You've always seemed like such a sweet young girl."

"Thank you."

Then as they walked Sister Davies asked Kristy what sort of things she liked.

"I don't know," Kristy said.

Well but what about books? What sort of books did she like?

"I don't really like to read," Kristy said. "I read for school and stuff, but I don't really like books. I like movies. And TV."

"Okay. So well what are some of your favorite movies."

"I don't know."

"You don't know what your favorite movies are?"

"I guess not."

"What's one? What's one favorite movie? I like *Lilo & Stitch*. Do you?"

"I don't know. I guess I don't really like movies."

Like this they continued for nearly half an hour. Between each door Sister Davies probing and Kristy giving answers that revealed either nothing or little about herself.

This wasn't a strategy.

It wasn't planned.

But Kristy didn't know what to say.

She didn't know *how* to say.

How to say that she loved *The Lion King*, but that her father said she couldn't watch it because Mufasa became a spirit, and spiritism was bad? How to say that she like *Edward Scissorhands* but that her parents said it was perverse because only God himself could create life (or his son, Jesus, could, but working only as an instrument of the father)? How to say that the answer to *What's your favorite music?*, when Sister Davies asked her what her favorite music was, was that she liked the classical stuff she heard in school but that her music teacher had recently played for the class on an old cassette deck a couple Tupac songs in the interest of historical precedent and she'd really liked those too?

Kristy couldn't share these things about herself.

She couldn't say she like Roald Dahl's *The Witches*, which she'd found on the shelf of her school's library three or four years ago and which was the only non-Jehovah's Witness-published book she'd ever read.

The correct answer to to *What's your favorite music?* should have been Song Number 15 of the book *Sing Praises to Jehovah*. Any song from that songbook would have been the correct answer, but Number 15 was a particularly lovely one: "Life Without End At Last."

They alternated doors, Kristy Kelly and Sister Davies. When it was Kristy's turn she, when she could get away with it, would only pretend to ring the doorbell, placing her finger on it but not depressing the button. "No one home," she would say after a few seconds, her head down, and Sister Davies would make a note of the house number so it could be tried again later. At doors without doorbells, where she had to knock audibly, Kristy prayed no one would answer.

After they'd completed one street, and then another, and then another, Sister Davies said: "I'm hungry. Are you hungry? And I could use a coffee and a bathroom."

KRISTY KELLY AND SISTER DAVIES went to a McDonalds downtown. Sister Davies bought herself a large coffee. To the coffee she added four packets of sugar and four containers of cream. She bought Kristy an orange juice. She bought them both an Egg McMuffin because the week's special was two Egg McMuffins for a dollar.

Sister Davies was a full-time volunteer preacher, a Pioneer. She made no money from her ministry. Her elderly parents each month sent her money from New Orleans, where they lived and where Sister Davies had been born and raised.

As they ate their sandwiches, Sister Davies told Kristy she wanted to study the Bible with her, to help Kristy draw closer to God, if Kristy wanted to.

Kristy's great-grandmother on her mother's side was one of the original Bible Students.

Bible Students, International Bible Students, Independent Bible Students—these were the names adopted in the late 1800s by the followers of Pastor Charles Russell, who left the Presbyterian Church at age thirteen to start a new religion, one independent from dogma and rhetoric, and wrote and published what was then called *Zion's Watchtower*.

Zion's Watchtower and Herald of Christ's Presence. Kristy's great-grandmother and thousands of others wore placards with the name and sold copies of the magazine for a nickel a piece in the streets of Pennsylvania. Kristy's great-grandmother married a phonograph operator and together they dedicated themselves to God.

IN THE EARLY 1900S THERE were schisms and divisions.

Charles Russell died.

His closest friend and disciple refuted his teachings, disseminating new ones to the rank and file.

Some Bible Students became Dawn Bible Students. Some, New Covenant Believers. Others, Layman's Home Missionaries.

Not everyone knows about these other groups, even though several of the groups still exist today, but I've done my research. I've always found history fascinating, and what history is more fascinating than your own? Some people, I've noticed, couldn't care less about their history.

In 1931, fifteen years after his death, Russell's most faithful students starting calling themselves Jehovah's Witnesses.

Kristy Kelly's great-grandmother died decades before Kristy was born, but her family talked about her often and nobly. Kristy's family was part of a legacy. Something big and eternal.

"WE HAVE SOMETHING TO TELL you," Kristy's mother said.

Her mother and her father sat in front of her on her bed where she was doing homework late into the night. Their eyes were red and her mother's cheeks were peeling.

Her mother tried to tell her whatever it was they had to tell her, but she choked and couldn't speak the words.

Her father put a hand on her mother's shoulder and looked at Kristy and said: "Your brother—"

Kristy's thought was that maybe her brother was dead. And she didn't know how to feel because she'd never been close to her brother but still she probably loved him.

"Your brother—" her father said again. But then he broke down too, like her mother—worse than her mother— and the words dried in his mouth.

Kristy Kelly's brother wasn't dead but he was dead to them all.

Her brother had listened to teachers who told him he was brilliant and had potential and would be wasting himself if he didn't go to college and get a degree and change the world. So he'd enrolled in the local university and his attendance at congregation meetings and family worship and his participation in the ministry had grown erratic, and last week he came home and told his parents he'd decided to move into the campus dorms. And when they pressed him he admitted to experimenting with drugs like marijuana and to having a girlfriend outside of The Truth.

The Truth is what one finds when one lives in accordance with Bible principles, when one dedicates oneself to God's organization. In The Truth there is brotherhood and worship and love. Sometimes people fall out of The Truth. Sometimes people stumble and fall right out.

Kristy's brother had met with a disciplinary committee—a team of congregation Elders—and the committee's decision was to disfellowship. Kristy's brother had moved out that morning while Kristy was at school. He hadn't said goodbye and because he was disfellowshipped she couldn't call and say it herself, even if she wanted to. At the next night's meeting they announced that her brother wasn't a Jehovah's Witness anymore so that the congregation would know.

So he wasn't dead but he was dead to all of them.

KRISTY WAS FIFTEEN THE SUMMER she was baptized. The water washed over her like a blanket of light and Holy Spirit.

She held her nose with one hand and held that arm's elbow with the other hand in the way she was instructed.

She was under the water for five infinite seconds, fully submerged. Her legs came up but one of the Elders in the pool caught them and held them under so that the water took all of her. Free fall.

When she came up, and after she toweled and changed into dry clothes, her mother and her father and Sister Davies joined her and snapped pictures and told her how proud of her they were. Her father gave her her own leather-bound Bible: purple with a gilded ribbon and gilded edges and gilded words on the cover. It was even inscribed, specially for her. Her father's wasn't inscribed. Her brother's hadn't been inscribed. But hers was. It said: *Property of Kristy Kelly.*

KRISTY ENTERED HIGH SCHOOL. SHE was fifteen and a half and wanted her learner's permit, but her parents insisted she needn't be in such a rush to grow up. They'd still drive her to school and congregation meetings and in the ministry. But she wanted freedom.

Freedom, they told her, was often a dangerous thing. Look at her brother.

IN A TENTH-GRADE BIOLOGY class they were learning about *homo Habilis* and neanderthals and all that came before.

These things weren't true, Kristy knew. But her conscience was comfortable with playing along, with learning only to dismiss once the class was over and the tests were taken. She took copious notes on humanity's genetic lineage, and on trilobites and troglodytes and fossils and ancient pre-human skulls that had supposedly been found in caves in Africa and South America. She answered test questions in the way expected of her.

I did not see Kristy Kelly much myself during this time. Even in those years when our education might have overlapped —she in eleventh grade and me in ninth—we weren't in the same building. My mother homeschooled me. I had my own braces now and Kristy Kelly's were long gone. At the Kingdom Hall on Thursday nights and Sunday mornings I watched her from several rows behind. On Saturdays when the Brother arranging groups for the ministry did his thing never did I end up in the same car as Kristy Kelly.

Kristy's biology teacher said they had to do this big project on the origin of man, complete with poster and diorama and five-page writeup.

This is where she drew the line. Where at her parents' and Sister Davies urging she decided to make a stand for her faith.

IN A LARGE CARDBOARD BOX Kristy Kelly built her very own Garden of Eden. It had little patches of astroturf for the green green grass, blue water made of Play-Doh, trees and bushes made from tiny samplings of real trees and bushes she'd clipped from her front yard with pruning sheers. Monkeys and anteaters and birds and butterflies and antelope and tigers. A big yellow sun that gave off so much light because her father had helped her wire it so.

There were no people in the diorama, but at the Garden's gates two golden cherubs stood, arms crossed, between them a flaming, spinning sword drawn and cut from an index card and held floating above the ground by an invisible piece of fishing line, for this diorama depicted a time after the fall of man.

THE BIOLOGY TEACHER FAILED HER.

"This is a fantasy," he said, gesturing in front of the entire class toward the cardboard box. "I teach a science class, not literature."

Kristy told her parents and they called the school and demanded to speak to the principal. The principal spoke to the teacher and the teacher said he'd be willing to issue a new grade if Kristy redid the assignment. Correctly this time, he said. Accurately.

Kristy's parents and Sister Davies told her the decision was hers but she should prayerfully consider which choice would make God's heart rejoice. She prayed and she prayed and she prayed, and she went to sleep. And in the morning with a strange sense of unease she went downstairs and found her parents drinking coffee and told them she wasn't going to redo the assignment.

The school board got involved and the local press got involved, and briefly Fox News and CNN picked up the story of the girl who had conviction in her beliefs and each reported on it in their own way. Because of all the attention, the school board had no choice but to "release the teacher from his contract" on grounds of religious discrimination.

Kristy Kelly's parents and Sister Davies and her fellow congregation members praised her for her stand. Even some of her school peers praised her, thought her bold. Others hated her for causing the termination of their favorite teacher.

Kristy Kelly told me this is really where she began to wonder.

In time she was asked to think about her future.

"Your grades are excellent, outstanding," her guidance counselor said. They sat in an office wallpapered with phrases like:

Lost time is never found again.

and

Enjoy the little things in life, for one day you will look back and realize they were big things.

and

Know first who you are; and then adorn yourself accordingly.

"If you don't start to think now about which colleges you want to apply to," the counselor said, "your chances of getting in drop dramatically. But right now you have all the chances in the world."

WHILE KRISTY WAS PREACHING ONE Saturday with Sister Davies, Sister Davies said: "What are some of your goals, Kristy?"

Kristy said, like she always did: "I don't know."

Kristy wasn't fake-pressing doorbells anymore. She pushed them firmly, but not without the unexpressed trepidation that comes from the prospect of talking with strangers. Or from the prospect of talking.

"Have you considered pioneering?"

"Maybe," Kristy Kelly said.

"Or what about Bethel service? There's no greater joy than serving Jehovah at the headquarters of his organization. No greater privilege, you know."

Bethel, from the Hebrew *Beth-El*, means "house of God". At that time the U.S. headquarters of Jehovah's Witnesses were located in Pennsylvania and in Walkhill, NY, and in Brooklyn. Brooklyn was where the Governing Body, God's spokesmen on Earth, lived. These days the whole operation is in the process of being moved to New Jersey. We, all of us, have donated a lot of money to make the move happen.

"Yeah, maybe," Kristy said. She depressed a doorbell and waited. The cover of the *Watchtower* in her hand had a painting of a woman superimposed over a war zone and said in bold font: GOD WILL END ALL SUFFERING. WHEN? HOW?

As HIGH SCHOOL PROGRESSED KRISTY Kelly became interested in things. She took the school's one-semester journalism course (a prerequisite for joining the school paper). She became fascinated with the concepts of human anatomy as discussed in a medical context, fascinated with bones and organs and systems and functions. Maybe she could study phlebotomy at a trade college after high school. She didn't mind the sight of blood. There were young sisters in neighboring congregations who were phlebotomists. They liked their work and they had plenty of time for the ministry.

Kristy decided she wanted to join the track team after attending a meet while writing a sample sports piece for her journalism class. She'd never been a very physical person, but her family ate well and she was trim and had always been fast. When they played volleyball at congregation picnics, she was quick and maneuvered well and her hits had power.

If only she could join the track team.

But she couldn't join the track team, and here's why:

"Bad associations spoil useful habits" –1 Corinthians 15:33, so the translation says.

THERE CAME A RUMOR FROM a congregation a few towns over:

One of the Elders there, a Brother long in his service to God (fifty years he'd been baptized; thirty years he'd been an Elder), had been fucking young boys.

That's how Kristy first heard it put, by her mother to her father: He's been fucking young boys.

"He's been fucking young boys!" her mother said when she read about the Elder's arrest in the paper. Kristy and her mother and her father were sitting around the dinner table. Another woman in the congregation had called Kristy's mother and told her the news that afternoon but her mother hadn't believed it until just now when she found it in black ink in the paper.

"Let's eliminate the language, huh?" her father said.

"But it says it right here. Right fucking here. Brother Buxton has been accused of having sex with a ten-year-old boy. It says, 'Buxton, a member of the Bridgeville Congregation of Jehovah's Witnesses, is believed to have been using his position of power within the church to engage in inappropriate sexual contact with children in the congregation for twenty years or more.' Twenty years! Boys *in his fucking congregation*!"

"I SAID CUT IT WITH THE LANGUAGE!"

The table rattled. The plates and silverware rattled.

"I'm sorry," Kristy's father said, breathing slowly. "It's horrible news, but the local bodies of Elders have been conducting our own investigation and—"

"And, wait," Kristy's mother said, "and so that means you *knew* about this. You *knew*?"

"Oh, come on, honey. You know I can't tell you about stuff like this. It's confidential."

"Oh no. Oh no no no. I am your *wife*. You tell me when there are things like this that could put our family in danger. You fucking tell me."

"Come on, honey. Please stop swearing."

"We have a daughter. We had a son. What if—? It's too horrible to even think about."

"Well, and besides, our investigations seem to indicate he didn't do it. He says it's untrue. There are no witnesses. Only one child says—"

Kristy ate her dinner. She didn't know Brother Buxton, she told me.

Kristy Kelly didn't join the track team.

She didn't join the volleyball team.

And after finishing her journalism course she didn't enjoy writing all that much, so she didn't join the school paper.

At the beginning of Kristy's senior year she found a flyer hanging on one of the school's puce walls above the water fountain just outside her math class.

The flyer said, in frilly bubble letters:

DO YOU ENJOY TRIVIA?
COME. TRY OUT FOR THE ACADEMIC QUIZ BOWL TEAM.
THIS THURSDAY IN THE ART ROOM
IMMEDIATELY AFTER SCHOOL

In the flyer's bottom right-hand corner was a little hand-drawn doodle of Albert Einstein.

Thursday was a congregation meeting night, but with the tryouts being right after school they wouldn't interfere. Kristy told her parents she needed to stay late on Thursday to meet with her math teacher about an extra credit assignment. Could they pick her up an hour later than normal?

"An hour," her mother said, "to talk about an assignment?"

"Yes, well, I'm not the only one with an appointment. I'm like third on his schedule that afternoon."

"Well okay then. But then you'll have to come home and get ready pretty quickly. Your father is conducting the theocratic school this Thursday, filling in for Brother Wallace. Brother Wallace's son is a nice young man, you know. And he's just a couple years older than you. Maybe you should get to know him. You'll be graduating soon."

"Maybe I could get my own car," Kristy said. "So you won't have to pick me up from school like this."

"Yes, well, maybe."

The quiz bowl team tryout went well. It turned out Kristy knew things. She didn't like to read much, but she was quiet and she listened and so she'd heard things, like that Sherlock Holmes' address was 221B Baker Street, and that the first four and largest of Jupiter's moons were discovered by Galileo, and that Earth's own moon was called Luna (and not, as her father insisted the time she'd told her parent that bit of trivia, "The Moon". "The moon is just the moon," he'd said. "But why wouldn't it have a name," she'd said. "Why would it," he'd said. "The sun doesn't have a name. It's the sun." "The sun's name is Sol, Dad." "Show me in the Bible where God names the sun Sol and the moon Luna, show me."), and that Robert E. Lee died of pneumonia in 1870, and that in George Lucas's original draft of *The Star Wars* Luke Skywalker was a girl named Starkiller.

"We meet on Tuesdays and Thursdays," the team's academic advisor told her. "Our first competition is in four weeks. Welcome to the team."

It seemed at first like Kristy joining the quiz bowl team would be a problem.

"But this is something I want to do," she said when her parents questioned the need for her to be on the team. "Not something I need. Just something I really want to do."

"Have you thought about how this will benefit you spiritually, Kristy?" her father said.

Kristy said she didn't get the point of the question.

Her father's face fell and for a second he looked as if he might cry. He produced from thin air his weatherbeaten legendary Bible and told Kristy to read with him 1 Corinthians 10:31. And he read: "'Therefore, whether you are eating or drinking or doing anything else, do all things for God's glory.' And think, too," he said, "about your fellow Brothers and Sisters, Kristy. What might they think about you participating in extracurricular activities? See Verse 32? 'Keep from becoming causes for stumbling to Jews as well as Greeks and to the congregation of God.'"

But Kristy knew this one, this scripture, and she pointed a retaliatory finger at Verse 29. She read aloud: "'For why should my freedom be judged by another person's conscience.'" And then she said: "This whole chapter is all over the place, Dad. Paul was just saying like whatever."

Kristy's mother's hand went to her mouth and she did that sobbing thing she always did.

In time they acquiesced.

She promised to miss no meetings, to preach every Saturday morning and every Sunday afternoon, to let neither school nor her new extracurricular activity interfere with her spirituality, with her relationship with God.

She asked them if she could learn to drive now. Still they were less than amenable to the idea. Safety, her mother gave as a reason. Too much freedom, was one her father cited, too much opportunity to do wrong things and end up like her brother. Danger.

But they acquiesced to this, too, after Kristy made her argument, an argument they could not dispute because it was their duty as Christian parents to support the spiritual goals of their children.

"But I've been thinking," Kristy's argument went. "I've been thinking when I graduate I want to start pioneering, like Sister Davies and the others. But so to do that I'll need to drive, and I'll need a car." And they consented.

Her father made, though, one request: that she not speak to others in the congregations about the quiz bowl team. He was an Elder, and it fell upon him to keep his Brothers, his flock, from stumbling, like Paul said.

"AN IMPORTANT QUESTION ABOUT TRUTH," Kristy Kelly told me not long before she left, "is who holds the monopoly on it? If you capitalize a word, does it become *your* word?"

Only now do I realize the question she was asking was: "Who is right?"

IN THE FOLLOWING MONTHS THE foundation of Kristy's spiritual life grew both shakier and stronger.

On Tuesdays and Thursdays after school she joined the rest of the quiz bowl team in the art room, where they practiced. Practice in the case of academic quiz bowl meaning ten to twenty minutes of asking each other random trivia questions, sometimes playing Trivial Pursuit in a structured way but usually just pulling cards and reading from them until someone shouted an answer. If the answer was wrong someone would good-naturedly call the person who'd answered an asshat. For the rest of the two-hour practice (which was rarely supervised by the team's faculty advisor), they'd goof off, watch videos on their phones, just generally (as Kristy put it when she told me) fuck around. "The two goth kids on the team spent a lot of time making out in the art room's shadowy pottery corner, near the kiln."

Kristy still joined the congregation on Thursdays, though, her mother picking her up two hours after school let out. Kristy would rush home and change from jeans into her formally modest skirt and blouse and join her parents for dinner. Her father would read a scripture and say a prayer and they'd eat the meal her mother had made and talk about their days. Her mother made for dinner things like roasted cornish game hens, brussels sprouts with walnuts and cranberries, rolls or croissants from a Pillsbury can, steamed carrots in margarine, pot roast, green beans, lasagna, spaghetti with homemade meatballs and Huntz sauce. She'd make a pot of coffee and they'd all drink a cup before heading together in the car to the Kingdom Hall. They arrived twenty minutes early to every meeting, "setting an example for the congregation."

After the two-hour meeting, with its dozen sermonish talks and two prayers and three songs, they stayed and socialized. Kristy's father sometimes had meetings with other Elders in the Hall's library, door closed.

They arrived home near ten or, on nights when her father's conferences were lengthy, ten-thirty. Kristy would take the remainder of the pot of coffee upstairs with her in a plastic thermos and do homework. Science, History, English, Math. Sums and equations. On Fridays she woke, tired but fulfilled in a certain way.

Every Monday, Wednesday, and Friday for three weeks she attended hour-long driver's ed classes.

And this is how her Saturday mornings went:

On Saturday mornings Kristy Kelly was woken by her mother's hurried knock on her bedroom's thin wooden door. The door didn't have a lock. Kristy Kelly's mother knocked and then opened the door and said: "Get up. Get dressed. There's coffee and waffles downstairs and we have to leave in forty minutes."

Kristy, when her mother knocked, would grab her comforter tightly and pull it high up on her neck, knowing the door was about to open. She worried as her mother opened the door that the room smelled like sex because she'd recently discovered masturbation and, though she was ashamed, had touched herself until she'd come the night before.

"I'm getting up," she'd say.

Sometimes her mother wouldn't shut the door again and Kristy would call after her "Hey! Mom! Shut the door", and her mother wouldn't hear her or would pretend to not hear her, and Kristy would have to keep the blanket tight around her body as she stood and shut the door herself. Kristy Kelly slept naked almost always. She didn't like her body, but she'd grown comfortable with its existence and with her existence in it. Mostly. Every month when her period came and she had to use tampons and panty liners she felt the loathing for herself God had told woman she would feel.

You are not a body with a soul; you are a soul, and you have a body. This was something she'd heard once, somewhere, but it didn't fit with what was supposed to be her philosophy.

Kristy dressed in the same sort of modest skirt she wore on Thursdays and in a loose blouse and sometimes in a knitted sweater. Sister Davies had taken up knitting and liked to knit sweaters and hats for people in the congregation. How she afforded yarn no one knew.

Kristy would go downstairs after running a brush through her hair and put a few waffles on a plate. They weren't homemade waffles—her mother just spent several minutes each Saturday morning toasting Eggos. The Eggos were usually cold by the time Kristy made it down. Kristy snuck real butter from the fridge and finished with Aunt Jemima's.

Her father would come into the kitchen then in a suit and tie and call for her mother, and he'd read a scripture and ask for comments and thoughts on the scripture before they all three of them left the house.

I'D SIT NEXT TO MY mom on Saturday mornings and hope to be put in the same preaching group as Kristy Kelly, but it happened only once and I couldn't think of a word to say to her as we went from door to door.

Charlie Wallace got to preach with Kristy Kelly a lot, though.

Charlie and I weren't exactly friends—he was three years older than me (a year older than Kristy Kelly)—but I admired him. *Respect* for him, is what I tell myself I had, because I'm afraid to admit it was something else. I was friends with Dan Herschel, and Dan Herschel was friends with Charlie Wallace, so Charlie and I hung in the same group sometimes. We played basketball with some of the other Brothers in our congregation on Saturday afternoons. During basketball Charlie mentioned he was kind of interested in Kristy Kelly and the older Brothers teased him, joked with him, said maybe he'd get hitched soon.

We still play basketball on Saturday afternoons. It's funny that I'm one of the older Brothers now (not old, just older than the teenagers, which feels old). I do the teasing now. "Maybe you'll get hitched soon," I say to the younger Brothers.

ACADEMIC QUIZ BOWL SEASON STARTED in a big way. The team's first match against another school was on a Tuesday evening. The tournament matches were hosted by a local weatherman and broadcast in place of *Jeopardy!*. Several people in the congregation tuned in and saw Kristy Kelly correctly answer question after question with her team. Kristy's father was embarrassed. He tried to make her drop the team, but she wouldn't do it. Who knows what kind of heat he took from the other Elders.

"YOU WERE REALLY GOOD TONIGHT," the captain of the quiz bowl team said.

"Thank you," Kristy said. She was standing outside the news station waiting for her ride.

"I'm having a party this weekend and I really think you should come. I really think you'd enjoy it."

"Thanks, but I don't really go to parties. I'm one of Jehovah's Witnesses."

"Oh, I know. And I think that's awesome. I respect a girl who has firm beliefs. I'm a Christian, too."

"Yes, well, but I don't go to parties, so."

"That's okay. But you're very beautiful, and I think you're interesting, and if you change your mind you should let me know."

KRISTY KELLY DIDN'T GO TO that party. And she didn't go to the next, or the next. The captain of the quiz bowl team invited her to a lot of parties, and she didn't go to them. She didn't tell her parents or Sister Davies about the parties, but she didn't go to them, either. And in not going to them a hole inside herself grew larger—it grew the size of all the things she might have experienced if she had gone to one of the parties. What would she have learned?

TOGETHER THEY WALKED FROM HOUSE to house, Charlie Wallace and Kristy Kelly.

"So, what are your plans when you graduate?" Charlie said.

Kristy could see, on the other side of the street, her mother and Sister Davies. She wondered what they were talking about, if they were talking about her and Charlie. They'd both mentioned Charlie to her, said he was a nice spiritual young man, and handsome too.

"I haven't exactly decided yet," Kristy said. "But I'm thinking about maybe pioneering. You graduated last year—how did you decide what to do?"

"Well, I though about Bethel service, you know. Imagine—working at the headquarters of God's earthly organization. Being an instrumental part of spreading The Truth to all corners of the world and stuff. But also my father's getting older, you know, and he wants to retire in a few years, maybe take the extra time to pioneer himself, with my mom. So I prayed about it. A lot. I prayed a lot. So but in the end I decided to stay, work with my dad, serve our local congregation, you know?"

"Yeah," Kristy said. She both admired this and didn't. She'd been thinking lately about what it would be like to be a doctor. She'd scored fantastic marks on her SATs. Her counselor was convinced she could get into many of the best schools, and numerous scholarships would be waiting for her. Kristy hadn't shared her scores with her parents. When they'd asked why she even wanted to take the SATs, with no plans of pursuing higher education, she'd said she was just curious.

She wondered as they walked what it would be like to hold Charlie's hand right now, but this wasn't the time, and it wasn't the place, and she didn't like him, just wanted to hold someone's hand.

THE ACADEMIC QUIZ BOWL CHAMPIONSHIP was on a Thursday at 7 PM the week of the semi-annual visit of the Circuit Overseer, who's kind of like an Elder but one appointed by the Governing Body itself, assigned to visit and measure and bolster the spritual health of dozens of congregations in a given area. You don't miss the Circuit Overseer's visit. His words come from the Governing Body, and the Governing Body is Christ's mouthpiece on Earth.

At dinner a week before, Kristy told her parents her team had made it to the championship match, that the match would be an hour long and taped in front of an audience and televised like the other matches but shown more than once, and that if her school won they might join the national tournament. "But it's next Thursday," she told them, "so I won't be in the match myself, I've decided."

"That's a wise decision," her father said.

"We're proud of you," her mother said.

THE DAY AFTER THE MATCH the team's captain found her as she was getting into the old four-door silver car her parents had just bought her as a gift "so you can drive the group in the ministry when you need to and so you can get a job after graduation."

"Kristy!" the captain called as he approached. "Kristy Kelly!"

She tossed her bag on the back seat and shut the door and turned around to meet him.

"I'm sure you heard we lost yesterday," he said. "I'm sure you heard we missed that last biology question."

She hadn't heard. She'd spent the day trying very hard to not care how the team had done. When she'd seen the Goth couple making out in the hallway by the auditorium she'd turned left so they wouldn't see her. She'd had a feeling, though, that they'd lost, because the principal hadn't made an announcement. He made an announcement every time a school team won something.

"No," she said.

"We did. We lost," he said. "And we might not have if you

were there. If you were there we almost definitely would have won. And it wouldn't even have been close."

For several seconds Kristy didn't respond. She felt bad about the loss and about the fact that she hadn't been there. Her bad feelings didn't stem from any sort of loyalty, from any sort of guilt. Kristy Kelly felt loyalty to no one, she'd come to understand, not to her God, nor to her team, not to her parents or herself. She was existing in the world. She didn't make choices. She didn't, she realized, standing by her car with him, feel bad.

"I'm sorry," she said. And then she took his shoulders in her hands and spun him. She pushed him against the car. She kissed him just to see what it felt like, a kiss. What it tasted like.

With wide eyes he accepted her apology and wiped her saliva from his lower lip.

She would not ever speak to the quiz bowl team captain again. In the hallways she would never meet his gaze, and soon he would stop gazing. By the next week he would become just a background actor, an extra, not even a character.

KRISTY KELLY DROVE. SHE DROVE up and down the hills of the long road to her house. She took the corners at moderate speed. She was comfortable driving but not very. The radio played "I Do Not Hook Up" by Kelly Clarkson. Kristy didn't hear it. Kristy was numb. There was in her ears a buzzing, a hollow hum that permeated her and made her teeth chatter. And as she pulled to the curb in front of her house the hum receded and gave way to a cold drum.

"DAD!" SHE CALLED WHEN SHE entered the house. She dropped her bag on the bench under the coat rack that hung on the wall in the foyer. "Dad?"

She took her shoes off. She placed them neatly side by side under the bench. Her father was never home when she got home unless he'd left work early. He wasn't off early today. Her mother wasn't in the kitchen or the living room.

Kristy took the stairs to her bedroom and hugged herself underneath a blanket.

HER MOTHER CAME HOME SOME time later and called for her and Kristy did not answer. Some time after that her mother knocked on her bedroom door and then opened it and said: "There you are. Are you okay?"

"I'm not feeling well," Kristy said. "I think I have the flu."

"Oh, well." Her mother crossed the threshold and sat on the bed and placed the back of her hand on Kristy's forehead. "You feel warm," she said. "You're sweating."

Kristy nodded.

"You should rest."

Kristy nodded.

In the morning they let Kristy sleep. They went preaching without her. Kristy prayed a lot while they were gone. She prayed and she watched television and she ate potato chips she found in the back of the pantry.

By the end of the day she'd decided it was just a kiss, and it wasn't like sex or oral sex or anything and it was stupid and she'd prayed a lot and God knew she was sorry and she didn't have to tell anyone and she felt much better. She existed again but maybe now more so.

WHEN I WAS VERY LITTLE I loved being sick on Saturdays or Sundays because it meant I could stay home and watch cartoons like other people.

KRISTY READ THE PIONEER APPLICATION. She answered the following questions, just like the top of the application instructed her to:

Have you been disfellowshipped or disassociated within the last five years?

Have you been reproved by a judicial committee for wrongdoing within the last five years?

Do you truly believe that spiritual food from Jehovah is being provided through the "faithful and discreet slave" class and that this "slave" class is using the Watchtower Bible and Tract Society as its legal agent?

She signed her name on the line provided.
Kristy Kelly.

THE MONEY FROM SISTER DAVIES' elderly parents had stopped coming, she told Kristy as they sat in the car. They were sitting in the car in the driveway of a house where Charlie Wallace and Dan Herschel were conducting a Bible study. The study would probably last an hour—most Bible studies did.

"Oh," Kristy said. "But why? Is everything okay?"

Sister Davies took a long slurp of the sweetened iced coffee she'd purchased from McDonalds on the way to the Bible study. "Well, so," she said after she was done slurping. "So I called my dad a week after the deposit didn't come through. I decided to wait a while, of course, when it didn't come, just in case it was coming late or there was a glitch or something. So I waited a week and it still wasn't there and so I called my parents and my dad told me they decided to stop sending me money."

"Yikes. Why?"

"That's the part that really breaks my heart. My dad said it's because I'm a JW."

"What? Why? That's horrible," Kristy said, but really she couldn't find it in herself to fault the old man.

"He said they've been concerned about me. Because I'm not married and because they saw a thing about Jehovah's Witnesses on *Dateline* or something and they think maybe it's a cult and they're worried about me."

"A cult?" A cult?

It's a common criticism. A lot of people think Jehovah's Witnesses are a cult. Or a sect. Maybe we're a sect in the strict definition of the word, but a cult? Kristy when she came to me near the end used the word. "Maybe we're in a cult," she told me. But we're not. I'm not in a cult. Kristy Kelly was *not* in a cult.

"But we're not in a cult," Kristy said to Sister Davies there in the car in the driveway.

"Well, and of course. I told him that. I said, 'Dad, do you know what a cult is?' And he was actually quiet for a minute. So I found that old *Watchtower* that talks about cults and read him the part where it explains that we aren't one. That cults control their members and but that we don't and you and I are here because we love God and Jesus. 'We're Christians just like you, Dad,' I said."

Kristy shifted on the car's back seat. "What did he say?"

"He said they were still worried. And then he told me they wanted me to get a job. That they wouldn't support me anymore."

"Hmm…"

"I'm almost fifty years old. What kind of job could *I* get?"

"Wow. I'm so sorry, Sister Davies."

And then Sister Davies started to cry. She was fifty years old and she started to cry in front Kristy Kelly. She started to cry because she didn't know how to take care of herself and she was fifty years old.

Kristy said: "I know how you feel, Sister Davies. I'm looking for a job too, for when I get out of school here soon, something that will let me pioneer and will support me but won't take too much time."

But Kristy wasn't fifty. Kristy had years to go.

Sister Davies looked toward the door of the house as if she hoped Charlie and Dan wouldn't suddenly come out and see her crying.

Kristy said the only thing she knew would help: "You'll find a job, Sister Davies. We'll find one. Jehovah provides for his happy people, and we need to throw our burdens on his shoulders."

SISTER DAVIES CALLED KRISTY KELLY at her home weeks later. Kristy's mother handed her the phone and said: "It's Sister Davies. She sounds excited."

"Hello," Kristy said.

Sister Davies had had a brilliant idea and she had to tell Kristy about it: they could clean houses together, Kristy and Sister Davies.

Sister Davies knew another sister in a nearby suburb's congregation who cleaned houses for just ten hours a week while pioneering, but she was pregnant now and wanted to give her clients to Sister Davies. They were wealthy clients. Big houses. Kristy and Sister Davies could split the work and split the profits. They could make $200-300 a week, each, easy.

So Kristy said: "Sure. Sounds like a great idea."

Sister Davies was broke and so was Kristy Kelly, so Kristy borrowed from her parents the initial capital needed to buy supplies: brooms and a mop and a mop bucket and sponges and a duster and a hand-held vacuum and various chemical agents.

BROTHER WALLACE ANNOUNCED FROM THE Kingdom Hall's platform that Kristy Kelly was now a Regular Pioneer. There was applause, and faces turned to look at her. I turned to look at her but I don't think she saw me. I don't think she saw anyone.

ON THE SATURDAY TWO WEEKS following the Thursday of that announcement, Kristy Kelly graduated. She attended the ceremony, wore her cap and gown. Hers, like the other girls', was red, and the boys' were blue—the school's colors. She turned the golden tassel. They'd asked her to give a speech since she was a valedictorian but she declined, said she didn't want to. She wasn't going to college and had no big secular plans so what exactly could she say that would be relevant to anybody listening. She did not tell her parents about being asked because they would have encouraged her to use the moment to give a witness, to speak about her faith, to do all things for God's glory. Each of the four other valedictorians thanked their gods in their speeches. Kristy just took the leather folio with the piece of paper that said *This is not your diploma. Your diploma will be mailed to you*, and turned the golden tassel. She hugged her parents and did not attend the parties.

ONE EVENING IN THE SUMMER that followed, while Kristy and her parents were eating dinner, the doorbell rang. Kristy stood and her mother stood and her mother said, "I'll get it."

"It's okay," Kristy said. "My legs are sore from sitting."

The bell rang again before she opened the door. When she opened the door she gasped.

"Hey, kid," her brother said. His hair was long and he was very thin and there were pimples on his patchily bearded face.

"Who is it?" Kristy's mother said, coming up behind her. And then her mother called for her father.

They asked Kristy in a choiceless way to go up to her room while they spoke. "I want to say—" she said, and they told her to go to her room.

At the top of the stairs she lingered for an hour. She could not always hear the conversation but sometimes there was shouting, and the gist of it was her brother wanted to come home. He was out of money and out of work and out of friends and just wanted to be with his family again.

"But…but…but…" Kristy's mother stammered at one point. "But you abandoned us! You turned your back on The Truth."

"But I'm sorry. But I want to come back," Kristy's brother said.

"That's bullshit," her mother said.

"Language, damn it!" her father said. And then: "I have to make a call."

Remnants grew cold on the dinner table.

THEY DID NOT TAKE HER brother back, not yet. He needed to show how sorry he was. He needed to mend his relationship with God before he could mend the ones with anybody else.

He got a job at Best Buy and cut his hair and shaved his beard and did not for a year miss a single congregation meeting. He arrived just before the opening song and prayer and sat in the back row, alone and quiet, and left just after the final song and prayer. He may have nodded to me once. I was putting away a microphone as he passed on his way to the exit.

He may have nodded, but I'm not sure. I nodded back.

KRISTY SAT IN THE MIDDLE of the middle row as the usher passed the plate of unleavened wafers to the first person, who passed it to the second, who passed it to the third. It came to her and she took it and passed it on.

This means my body.

The usher was Charlie Wallace. He was a Ministerial Servant now, just a step below his father.

They did the same with glasses of wine as with the plate of bread. Passing, passing, passing.

This means my blood.

KRISTY KELLY AND SISTER DAVIES did not usually clean the houses together. Each her own house they cleaned them. In this way between them they cleaned six or seven houses weekly.

CHARLIE WALLACE SAT NEXT TO her and smiled.

She smiled too and said: "Hi, Charlie."

Charlie shifted in the seat as if this was something he'd never done before (which it was). "I like you, Kristy," he said.

"Thanks. I like you too," she said.

"I like you a lot, though. I, um, well I admire and respect you and so. Well…"

"Yes?"

"Well so I would like the opportunity to know you better. To…to…to get to know you better."

"I'd like to go out with you too, Charlie," she said.

Charlie sighed as if he hadn't expected a positive answer.

I WON'T LIE: THERE'S LITTLE choice when it comes to who you marry in The Truth. You almost always end up married to someone you grew up with. Someone your own age or close to your own age, someone from the same congregation. If there's no one your age in your congregation and you're a woman, maybe you marry someone older than you, significantly older even. Kristy's brother married a girl twelve years younger than him, a girl born the same year he was baptized. If you're like me maybe you get the privilege of serving the organization somewhere far away for a few months (until the money you've saved to serve somewhere far away runs out) and you marry a respectable sister from Puerto Rico and you ask her to come back home with you and together you serve God and you've never really had adventures but it seems like you have, for a little while.

You often marry young. You can't have sex before you marry so you marry young. You don't date early, though. You date when you're ready to marry.

I married my Puerto Rican wife when I was twenty and she

was twenty. Our wedding night was awkward, if you want to know the truth, but you get into the rhythm quickly.

ONE OF THE HOUSES KRISTY cleaned was owned by a crunchy middle-aged woman and her husband, and the woman had jewelry.

In the master bedroom, which Kristy vacuumed weekly, a few feet from a crimson-blanketed bed and next to a door that led to an ornately chromed master bath with his and her sinks, was a wooden vanity.

Kristy stared at the vanity while she vacuumed. She had a vanity of her own in her own room—her mother had given it to her many years before—but she wanted this one. While she vacuumed she imagined this one in her room. This one had three mirrors: one in the center and one at an adjustable angle on each side, and the mirrors on the sides had hooks, and necklaces and lockets and pendants and pendula hung from the hooks. The vanity had shelves, too, for earrings and garnets. The shelves could be stacked or they could be unstacked like stairs. Their linings were velvet the crimson of the bedspread. Next to the vanity was large bottle of jewelry-cleaning solution.

When Kristy Kelly was vacuuming the bedroom she would turn the vacuum off and touch the surface of the vanity for a while.

When she vacuumed these houses Kristy was careful to take her shoes off and make only straight lines on the carpet.

"I GOT A CALL FROM one of our clients this afternoon," Sister Davies said over the phone. "She said her wedding ring went missing and she wanted to know if you'd seen it while you were cleaning."

Kristy held the cordless receiver to her ear. "Oh," she said. "No, I don't think so. Well, who was it? Which client, I mean?"

"It was just Mrs. Taintor from the house on Elm. I told her you probably hadn't seen it."

"No. No, I don't think I saw it anywhere."

"See, that's what I told her. And well, you see, she said maybe you took it, she said."

"Sister Davies, I would never—"

"And, see, that's what I told her. Told her we follow the Bible and wouldn't ever take something from her home."

"Okay. So what did she say?"

"So she said she was going to ask you. And I told her to let me do it."

"I would never. I didn't take it."

"Oh, I know."

The humming was back, the humming that backgrounded everything, but it was fainter than before.

"So I'm thinking maybe we should fire her?" Sister Davies said.

"What? What do you mean?"

"As a client. Remove her house from our list."

"Oh. Um, I guess."

"Okay. So."

"So." Kristy shifted the phone to her other ear. "Actually, no," she said. "Let's keep her."

"Really?"

"Yes. I'll—I should talk to her. I wouldn't want to leave things in any bad way."

"Well, okay then. I'll tell her you haven't seen it, and that you'll be by to clean, as per usual."

"Great. I think that's the best thing to do."

WHEN KRISTY PULLED UP TO the house on Elm there was a police car in the driveway and she thought about driving on and never coming back.

"This is her," the woman said when Kristy entered through the front door. 'This is the girl who took my ring."

But when Kristy told the officer she was a Jehovah's Witness, and Christian, and that she lived by Bible principles, the cop turned to the woman and laughed and said, "Don't you know about Jehovah Witnesses, ma'am? They're the most honest people you'll ever meet. They would never steal. We could learn a lot from them, you and I and most everybody else."

Kristy went home and called Sister Davies and told her it was probably a good idea to fire the client after all.

WHEN KRISTY KELLY TOLD ME this part of the story I asked her if she *had* taken the ring.

She looked at me and said: "Does it even fucking matter?"

KRISTY AND CHARLIE'S FIRST OFFICIAL date was at Buffalo Wild Wings on a Tuesday night when you could get wings and drumsticks for a special price. Something like sixty cents a piece for the wings and drumsticks.

Dan Herschel and I were there because Kristy and Charlie needed at least one chaperone. Charlie had asked Dan to tag along and he said he would and Charlie said Kristy would ask one of the other women in the congregation to come too so it wouldn't be just she and Charlie with Dan sitting there the whole time awkwardly.

But there were no other women in the congregation Kristy's age, and she didn't want to ask one of the older single ones, not even Sister Davies, because she saw them most mornings in the ministry, she said. So Charlie asked me to come, too, and we all agreed Dan and Charlie and I being there would be less awkward for Kristy than just she, Charlie, and Dan would have been for Dan.

Kristy sat next to Dan on one side of the table and Charlie

sat next to me on the other. This way I could see Charlie's hands and Dan could see Kristy's, and we could all in good conscience enjoy dinner, knowing Kristy and Charlie weren't doing under the table things they shouldn't be. The heart is treacherous and the flesh is weak, after all, says the scripture.

But we couldn't see their feet.

Under the table Charlie ran his foot across Kristy's foot. Kristy ran her foot along Charlie's feet.

Kristy looked at the menu and when Dan said "Let's all share one of those large orders of wings" and Charlie said to Kristy "What would you like?" she said "That's fine."

"What flavors should we get?" Dan said.

"I like that mango habanero," Charlie said.

"Says here they can split the flavors up to three ways," Dan said. "I like spicy garlic."

"Spicy garlic is good," Charlie said. "What would you like, Kristy?"

"That's fine," Kristy said. "Spicy garlic is fine."

The waitress came and asked if we were ready and we all ordered Cokes. "We need a few more minutes to decide on food," Charlie said.

"I like mango habanero," I said.

"We're already getting those," Dan said. "We still need one more flavor."

"I know," I said. "I was just saying that I like those, so we should get them."

"We are."

"What about these ranch?" I said.

"Ranch is good," Charlie said. "What do you think, Kristy?'"

Kristy tugged at her jeans. "Ranch is good," she said. She looked at the menu but she was just pretending.

"I'm not a big fan of ranch wings," Dan said, "but I can just eat the other two."

"But we should get flavors everyone likes," Kristy said, putting down her menu.

Everyone nodded.

"Who says we need to get three flavors just because we can?" Kristy said.

Everyone laughed. How silly we'd been. Just because we could.

When the waitress returned with our Cokes Dan ordered a large order of spicy garlic and mango habanero. He also ordered two baskets of potato wedges with cheese. Charlie ordered ranch dressing for dipping in lieu of ranch wings but the waitress told him dressings were extra tonight because the wings were so cheap, so Charlie said never mind to the dressing.

Kristy unwrapped her straw and then placed it in her drink. "Great job reading the *Watchtower* Sunday, Charlie." She bumped her knee into Charlie's knee under the table but we could not see it.

"Thanks," Charlie said. "I was really nervous. How did that Bible study you accompanied Sister Davies on go this morning?"

"It went well. Sister Davies thinks she could progress far once she gets past her family's opposition and starts attending meetings."

"That's great to hear," Charlie said. "Really really great."

Dan and I watched one of the big TVs on the wall. There was a college football game happening over there. One of the teams had the ball.

Wings would be difficult to eat on account of my braces, but I didn't tell anyone that.

After dinner the plan was to go see *The Dark Knight Rises* on one of the IMAX screens downtown. Kristy sat next to Charlie during the movie. Charlie, Dan, and I were in awe at the film. The costumes were cool. The action was cool. The protagonist climbing out of the literal prison of his soul was so cool.

"How'd he get back to the city so fast?" Kristy whispered near the climax. And her asking that kind of ruined the whole thing for me.

During the movie Charlie's hand found its way to Kristy's knee. Even in the darkness of the crowded theater her blush was visible—in fact it was more apparent than it might normally have been, enhanced by the glow of the fifty-foot curved screen. Kristy with hesitation and excitement and a little bit of guilt put her hand on top of Charlie's, and when his moved slowly up her thigh, higher than his leg at dinner had been physically capable of going, her hand moved with it, like a hand on a Ouija board (which as Witnesses we never played with) moving from letter to letter she moved with him, spelling out a dark message, unaware but secretly aware she was just in control as he was.

When I was very young I was curious about Ouija boards. How did the spirits work them, I wondered? And why did those spirits need a Hasboro toy to communicate with the rest of us? Why not use Monopoly?

I saw Charlie's hand stop in a questionable place, but not *so* questionable. This was dangerous maybe, but was it wrong? Kristy's hand rode his all the way there. Unlike under the table at dinner I watched this happen. I *felt* this happen. I felt Charlie touching Kristy, and I could feel Kristy touching Charlie also.

The movie ended and we all four of us walked along the river. Dan and I held back. A significant problem with chaperones is that, while the arrangement prevents any sort of uncleanness, it makes it very hard to be alone, to talk and share with each other things you may not want to share with your chaperones. I don't know if chaperones really help all the much, to be honest—there are stories where multiple couples chaperoned each other on dates and they all just had an orgy. Whole congregations were party to some of these orgies, according to the stories, and when the guys at Bethel heard they dissolved them, the congregations, to protect the good name of the organization. But, I don't know, these are just rumors.

Forty feet ahead of Dan and I in the moonlight Charlie and Kristy kissed. I asked Dan if we should say anything because this was only their first date and surely they weren't planning marriage yet.

"We don't need to say anything," Dan said. "It's not our business."

"Yeah," I said, "but maybe we should just let an Elder know so Charlie and Kristy can be counseled if they need to be."

"No," Dan said. "It isn't our business and we should let them be."

But still I wondered. I was also a little jealous. I don't know which one I was jealous of. I felt more jealous than guilty.

Kristy and Charlie held hands as they walked along the river for the rest of the evening.

A LITTLE OVER A MONTH later Kristy Kelly was reproved, which meant she'd done something wrong, like had oral sex or smoked a cigarette or something, and was very sorry and had begged for God's forgiveness, and we could still talk to her but should be careful and consider her not the best association until the reproof was lifted. The reproof meant also she was no longer a pioneer.

An announcement to this effect was made for Kristy Kelly but not for Brother Charlie Wallace.

The circumstances of the reproof were part of the story that Kristy Kelly told me. In fact, the reproof was pretty much the final part of the story.

After their first date Kristy Kelly and Charlie Wallace decided they were officially dating. Dating, then, obviously, with a view to marriage, it could be assumed.

Kristy thought Charlie was a good guy and a handsome young man. She liked that he was a Ministerial Servant and had assignments in the congregation and led the group in the ministry on Wednesday mornings, and that he had a solid job with his father's construction company, a job from which he could take Wednesday morning off so he could lead the group in the ministry.

In the following weeks they went together to all the congregation functions: picnics and bowling and dinners. They sat together at the meetings.

One Sunday evening they got a group together to go swing dancing at a local school where there were swing dancing lessons. No one had swing danced before, but Kristy and Charlie thought it would be fun and convinced others it would be too. The lessons involved everyone present dancing with each other in turn. Kristy danced with Dan and he stepped on her feet. She danced with me and I picked the steps up better and more quickly than I expected. Sister Davies was there and she was having trouble picking up the steps so Kristy offered to show her, to dance with her, but while they were dancing Sister Davies said, "I don't think I like this, two sisters dancing together. It ain't right." So Kristy handed Sister Davies off to Dan. When Dan, who still didn't know what he was doing and couldn't lead, put his hand on Sister Davies' shoulder, Sister Davies freaked out and decided she didn't want to be there and left.

"They're right," Charlie said to Kristy a couple days later after his father had pulled him aside and counseled him. "Dancing at a school like that isn't very appropriate for Christians. We shouldn't have gone."

"Why not?" Kristy said.

"It was just worldly people there. Not Jehovah's Witnesses. It wasn't really a Christian thing."

This was probably exactly what his father had told him. Kristy wondered what Charlie's own thoughts were. If he had any.

"I think I saw people smoking marijuana on the steps outside the school," Charlie said. "And some kids that probably weren't twenty-one were drinking."

"I didn't see that," Kristy said.

"All I'm saying is I need to set an example—we need to set an example—in the congregation."

"Yeah, okay."

"And besides, there's a lot of other stuff we can do. We should get some people together to sing kingdom songs and I'll play the guitar."

Kristy liked that Charlie played the guitar, but she never heard him play anything interesting. "Yeah, okay," she said.

"Okay?"

"Yeah, okay. That sounds fun."

"You know, I really like you Kristy. I admire how spiritually strong you are. I'm glad we're dating."

CHARLIE DID NOT KISS KRISTY again after their first date for weeks, and she was disappointed. She liked kissing him. It wasn't just the fact that she'd been kissed that interested her but the actual act of kissing Charlie, of tasting with her lips and her tongue his specific lips and tongue.

At night she touched herself in the secret privacy of her bedroom and thought about kissing Charlie. She stroked herself and thought about his tongue in her mouth. She wanted to suck on his tongue, really kiss him in a way that was wrong and perverted. She pinched her nipples with one hand and with the other stroked herself while in her mind Charlie's shirt came off. Charlie worked for his father's construction company. He was well muscled, probably, his skin dark.

Kristy brought herself off and just as she reached climax plunged her fingers deep inside herself.

And immediately after, while she lay there shaking shallowly, sleepily, she was overwhelmed with the dirty thing she'd done. She was a dirty thing. A displeasing thing in the eyes of her God.

She got up from bed and pulled *Questions Young People Ask* from a shelf. She turned to the chapter on masturbation. The chapter told her she was not a bad person because of what she'd done. Though she'd made Jehovah sad by masturbating, she'd in no way lost His favor.

As the book said to do, she prayed. Ask forgiveness, it said, and seek the council of a parent or an Elder or a trusted older one in the congregation.

So Kristy prayed herself to sleep and resolved to speak with her mother in the morning, or maybe with Sister Davies in the ministry.

Each night Kristy Kelly did this.

ONE NIGHT ABOUT FOUR WEEKS after they started dating, Kristy invited Charlie to her house for dinner and a movie. Kristy's parents weren't going to be home, but she didn't tell Charlie that, but Charlie should have asked her, and he shouldn't have gone to her house.

Kristy was almost nineteen now and the more she thought about it the more she felt that being alone with another human being was a fundamental right, even if that other person was a man. Of course, there was danger here. If someone found out Kristy and Charlie had been alone in a house together, and if that person told the Elders, there would be discipline. Even if nothing physical had happened there would be discipline, because to be alone together was to invite temptation. The flesh is weak—remember? If you were alone with a person of the opposite sex, there was the extreme potential something had gone down. Something unclean and brazen and maybe even fornication. And what witness was there to deny uncleanliness except the sinners? And how could the sinners by their very nature be believed?

There is a flaw in this logic, though, I know, and that flaw is homosexuality. What if two lesbians were alone together? What if two gay men were alone together? What if *I* was alone with Charlie and I had feelings for him or he had feelings for me? Sure, homosexuality is a sin in the first place, but there are gays and bisexuals in God's organization who just don't act on their lust—I know this. They don't come out or give in, because well…because how could they?

Whence comes temptation?

Charlie arrived with his guitar and a six pack of Diet Coke. "Where is everybody?" he asked when he stepped into the foyer.

"What?" Kristy Kelly said.

"Your parents, where are they?"

"They, um, aren't here," Kristy said, "but I didn't think that would be a big deal."

"No, I guess it's okay," Charlie said. "But we…I don't know."

"I just haven't seen you in a few days," Kristy said. "You weren't out Wednesday morning—"

"My dad and I had an early job. I told you."

"No, I know. It's okay. I just wanted to hang out."

They baked a frozen pizza and watched *The Bourne Identity* on DVD while they drank the Diet Cokes. Kristy sat next to Charlie on the sofa, close to him, close enough to feel heat from his body but not close enough to touch.

"I forgot how violent this movie is," Charlie said around a mouthful of cardboard crust.

Kristy, being honest with herself, didn't know what she'd expected tonight. She'd invited Charlie knowing the possibility of doing something wrong was there. But she knew that, if she did something wrong, she'd feel horrible about it after, and knowing she'd feel guilty was enough, she'd been sure, to keep her from crossing any sort of line. From crossing that line she'd for years now been wondering what it would be like to finally cross.

"I've really been noticing things like that ever since I became a Ministerial Servant," Charlie said. "It's hard to be exemplary, and nobody's perfect except for Christ, of course, but I think I can do better with a lot of things. I've been thinking of getting rid of—"

Kristy Kelly kissed Charlie then, first at the edge of his mouth and then, when he turned with wide eyes, his lips. She liked lips and wanted to feel them again.

Charlie pulled back. "We shouldn't do this," he said. "I told my dad last time we kissed and he reminded me what 1 Corinthians 6:18 says."

Kristy sat back. He'd told his dad last time? And had he told his dad how he'd slid his hand up her leg? "Okay," she said. "You're right. I—"

"No, it's my fault. I shouldn't have stayed here. We both know better than this."

"Are you going to tell your father about this time, too?"

"I…I guess not," Charlie said. 'But I should go. I really like you, Kristy, and—"

"I really like you too."

"Good. And I don't want to jeopardize my relationship with you."

"Me either," Kristy said.

She should have shown Charlie to the door then, or maybe he should have up and left of his own free will, but that's not what happened.

Kristy's hand was on Charlie's thigh—she'd put it there to support herself when she'd leaned in for the kiss—and it seemed like such a small thing to move it only a few more inches before he left. She brushed it against the denim between his legs and the denim grew outward. Charlie's hands moved then, too, moved her hand over the bulge in the denim, moved her hand faster. For a minute that was all they did, but then his hands left her hands and pulled at his zipper, pulled his gray briefs down, and pulled Kristy's head onto him, her mouth onto him.

Kristy Kelly felt Charlie grow inside her mouth and she moved her head, bobbing it in a way that made her neck stiff but made Charlie stiffer. It wasn't apparent how long the whole thing lasted, but Kristy breathed through her nose and when Charlie pulled her down harder onto him she held her breath and choked on the spit that formed in the back of her throat and she kept on going. She heard him grunt and it made her stronger. She didn't care that this didn't make her feel good the way stroking herself did. Lust had taken over. Lust or something else and how could this be wrong?

Charlie grunted louder than before and came inside her mouth. She didn't move. Didn't swallow. Didn't close her lips.

It's amazing how fast that guilt found her, just like when she masturbated.

"You bitch!" Charlie said.

Kristy was on the floor. He'd pushed her violently after he came, throwing her off him and to the ground. Her elbow hit hard and sent a shockwave through her arm.

"You slut," he said. "I can't…I can't believe I…I can't believe you just made me…"

She lay there forever. She heard the door open and close and the tears started falling. An eternity later she heard the door open again and close again and when her mother walked in she'd managed to pull herself onto the couch and sat there very very still, watching the movie's credits role by.

"Who's guitar is this?" she distantly heard her father ask from the foyer.

SHE THOUGHT THE ELDERS WOULD be kind to her. They'd been kind to her brother, she'd heard, and it was his own lack of repentance that had forced them to reluctantly disfellowship him from the congregation. They'd been *so pained*, she'd heard.

But that's not how it happened for her.

In the little library off to the side of the Kingdom Hall's main auditorium Kristy sat. She sat at a small table, a smaller version of the table on the stage in the main auditorium where sisters sat, speaking to each other, two of them, when they had parts in the meetings on Thursday nights, speaking to each other because Sisters weren't allowed to teach the congregation, only each other. Something Saul of Tarsus had said after the spirit of Christ Jesus had assaulted and blinded him on the Road to Damascus and he'd become a new man—once a persecutor of Jews and Christians he was renewed by faith, repentant of his old, evil ways, the way Kristy was repentant now.

She sat surrounded by books, new books and old. Old books

written by long-dead men. Books Kristy's great-grandmother would have studied and considered gospel in the early days.

She sat in front of three men who said God would reveal to them the condition of her heart and help them decide her fate. Prayerfully they would decide it.

"We need to know what happened," Brother Jones said, speaking around his walrus mustache.

Kristy wept. "I'm sorry. I'm sorry," she said.

Brother Jones exchanged glances with Brother Wallace. "Kristy," Brother Wallace said, "first we need to understand exactly what happened."

Brother Jones and Brother Wallace were on this disciplinary committee because they knew Kristy well. Since she was a child they'd known her, and Brother Jones had been an Elder at least that long. Brother Jones had been in the pool during her baptism. The third Elder in the room was Brother Quincy, a Brother in his thirties recently appointed—he didn't speak once during the interrogation. Kristy's father, despite his eldership, was not on the committee, for reasons given as "I'm too close to the situation—you're my daughter" when she asked him why he couldn't be there for her. There was no mention of the fact that Charlie was Brother Wallace's son.

Charlie wasn't here. He'd had his own hearing.

"Didn't…didn't Charlie tell you?" Kristy said, looking through red eyes at Brother Wallace. The part of her that didn't feel dirty—a part small but larger than she would have expected —wanted to stare a challenge into his heart.

Brother Jones sighed. "Kristy," he said.

"I…performed oral sex on Charlie," Kristy said.

Brother Quincy wrote something in a spiral notebook.

Each Elder held a Bible between his legs.

Kristy had been asked to bring her Bible but she'd forgotten it. When she saw theirs she'd pulled one from the library shelves.

"Did Charles perform oral sex on you?" Brother Jones asked.

"Charlie said he didn't," Brother Wallace said.

"You know we have to ask her," Brother Jones said. To Kristy he said: "Did Charles—Charlie—perform oral sex on you?"

Kristy shook her head. She sniffed. "No."

"Did he fondle your breasts?"

"No."

"Did he touch your vulva?"

"*No.*" Guilt welled up again in Kristy. It warred with violation.

"Was there penetration?"

"I…"

"Did Charlie penetrate you?"

"My mouth."

"Did he penetrate you vaginally? Anally?"

"No. No!" Kristy said. "My clothes were on."

"Okay. And did you touch yourself while you were performing oral sex?"

"My clothes were on!"

"Through your clothes?" Brother Jones said.

"No!" Kristy gave way again to sobs.

"Take your time," Brother Wallace said. "Do you need tissues?"

Kristy nodded and sobbed and felt filthy. No one moved to get her tissues.

The three Elders had started the tribunal with a prayer for guidance and wisdom.

"Kristy," Brother Jones said, "we'd like to share a scripture with you. Is it okay with you if we do that? Why don't you turn to it in your…in that Bible there. It's Acts chapter 3 verse 19. Why don't you read it for us."

Kristy tried to read it but failed to speak the words out loud.

Brother Jones read it: "'Repent, therefore, and turn around so as to get your sins blotted out.'" When he finished reading he said, "So you see the need for repentance. You see what Jehovah said there."

Kristy nodded.

"Then now let's read another. Jeremiah 31:19. It says: 'For after my turning back I felt remorse; after I was made to understand I struck my thigh in grief. I was ashamed and humiliated, for I bore the reproach of my youth.'"

Kristy sniffled.

"Have you prayed to Jehovah, Kristy?" Brother Jones said. "Have you poured your heart out, have you 'struck your thigh in grief' over your sin?"

And then Brother Wallace said, "Sister Kelly, are you sorry you've sinned against God? Are you sorry for what you've done to my son?"

They told Kristy to wait in the auditorium while they prayerfully considered the matter.

For fifteen minutes she waited. For thirty. For forty-five.

Brother Jones found her and asked her to rejoin them in the library.

They told her they'd reached a decision. They didn't use the word verdict, but to her that's what it was.

No one can judge except me, says the scripture.

They had Kristy read along with them another scripture, this one about keeping the congregation clean. They told her they believed she was genuinely sorry for what she'd done. But, they said, disciplinary action must still be taken. The congregation must be kept clean.

I DON'T KNOW WHY KRISTY Kelly came to me. I mean, why me?

I asked her why me and she said, "Why not you? I know you, but I don't know you so well that any of this will be difficult to say."

Maybe I wasn't real to her. She told me that nothing was real to her—nothing ever had been—but maybe that was a lie and everything was real but me. Or maybe she was telling the truth. Or maybe, by my very minor role in the whole of her existence, I was the only thing real enough for her. I don't know.

We didn't see Kristy Kelly for a while after they announced her reproof. She wasn't there the night they announced it. She wasn't there for weeks after. She didn't go out in the ministry and she didn't come to meetings and nobody heard from her. When I asked her mother where she was her mother told me Kristy was at home. That she was sick. She was very very sick, her mother said.

And then one day she called my house. I guess I was seventeen at the time, if my math is right. She called my house and my mother picked up and told me it was Kristy Kelly on the phone.

"Hello?" I said. For some reason my hands were shaking.

"Hey," Kristy said. Her voice was small. "Can I tell you some things?"

"Okay," I said.

I hadn't even known she'd had my number.

SHE TOLD ME EVERYTHING ABOUT herself. Everything that had ever happened to her or that she'd ever done or felt, as if this was the only chance she'd ever have to tell it to anyone.

And at the end she said: "I don't really know that I believe anymore."

"YOU HAVE TO HAVE FAITH," I told her. "We have to have faith."

"But what does that mean?" she said.

"You know what it means," I said. "Hebrews 11:1 says that faith is—"

"YOU'RE NOT LISTENING TO ME!" she said. "I know what the scripture *says*. But what does it *mean*? It's nonsense. Words strung together. An illusion of any sort of substance."

I DID WHAT I DID next because I was helping her. Because I cared about Kristy Kelly and had cared about her since I was six years old and she was eight and she had braces. You don't leave a lost friend behind—you send a search party.

So I told Brother Wallace about Kristy, about some of the things she'd said to me. Not all of them, not most of them, but I told him about her doubts, about the lack of confidence I'd heard in her voice. I told him maybe he could talk to her, help her out.

He smiled and put a hand on my shoulder. I swear the gesture was full only of warmth and love.

He said thank you and something about apostasy I don't remember the specifics of.

I DON'T REALLY KNOW WHAT happened after that because I never talked to Kristy Kelly again, but a little while later she was gone. They told us from the platform she was gone. Her father resigned as an Elder. He needed to focus on his family before he could protect the congregation.

I LAST SAW KRISTY KELLY at her brother's wedding. A few people didn't go to the wedding because they'd heard she was going to be there. Her brother and his fiancée couldn't hold the ceremony at the Kingdom Hall because Kristy was invited, so they held it in a ballroom of a local Holiday Inn.

She came only for the ceremony. She stood in the very back and was quiet. She didn't applaud when her brother kissed his bride, the kiss a light respectful peck. She left when it was over. No one ever acknowledged that she was there—not even her brother, who'd invited her—but I remember her being there. I'm acknowledging it now.

I've Googled her name a few times in the years since, but all a search for "Kristy Kelly" returns is old academic quiz bowl headlines from local newspapers. I suppose that means she's alive out there somewhere, right? Because if she was dead there'd be news.

Her family never speaks of her.

DO I FEEL BAD?

I mean, yes, I do, a little. I sympathize with Kristy Kelly. I didn't do things right either. I've told you about her failings but I've told you almost nothing of my own.

I've had doubts like she did. I think we all have. Even now I have them. Especially now.

But where else would I go if not here?

Where else can we go?

ABOUT THE AUTHOR

Shawn was born in San Diego, California, in 1990, where he lived until he was seven. He was raised as one of Jehovah's Witnesses and left the religion when he was twenty-two.

In high school, he won several awards both as a writer for and editor-in-chief of his student newspaper, prompting him to study journalism before deciding that his passion for writing was better directed at fiction.

He is the author of four books: *The Flute Player*, *Brand-Changing Day*, *Particles*, and *The Assured Expectation of Things Hoped For*. He is the editor-in-chief of Asymmetrical Press, a publishing company for the indie at heart.

Shawn currently lives in Helena, MT, with his wife and their cats Oliver and Worf.